My horny secretary

Anna Paul

Table of contents

Chapter1

Rachel hurled down the collector and murmured softly, "Numbskulls, the world is brimming with idiots!!!"

She rifled through the huge number of papers that were spread all around her enormous work area, lastly in irritation punched the radio button and requested, "Jane, get in here,

I really want some assistance!" Jane put away the letter she was composing and went straightforwardly into Rachel's office.

"What's up chief?" she asked brilliantly. "You recall the Cambridge record?" Rachel asked without gazing upward.

"I know it's here in some place, yet for the existence of me I can't track down the damn thing!"

Jane slipped back out the entryway and recovered the required record from her own work area and returned while inquiring, "Is this the thing you're not kidding?"

"Thank god," Rachel said while drooping once more into her seat, "I was sure that I had left it at home.

" Jane strolled over to the rear of the work area and started scouring Julia's shoulders while murmuring delicately, "I think you want a break, you're so tense!"

Rachel shut her eyes briefly and moaned, "I don't have any idea how that fool Eric at any point became a lawyer, on the off chance that I at any point have the desire to engage with him again shoot me!"

"We should not ponder him," Jane said soothingly, "as a matter of fact, isn't there no time like the present you went potty?"

"Ohhhhh, you're correct," Rachel answered while getting to her feet. "I in all actuality do need to go!"

The two ladies vanished into Rachel's confidential washroom, whereupon Rachel pulled up the fix of her skirt, permitting Jane to pull down her frilly white undies cautiously!

"Mmmmm," Jane murmured, "I don't really accept that I've at any point seen these, they're exceptionally beautiful!"

"Much obliged," Rachel answered while sitting her stout base on the latrine seat, "I just got them at the end of the week.

" With her legs spread wide, Rachel moaned as Jane delicately opened the lips of her easily shaved vagina and held them separated while a surge of hot brilliant pee soared from her full bladder!

Chapter2

"Feeling significantly improved?" Jane asked delicately. ", yes," Rachel said, "such a ton better!"

As the last piece of pee dribbled from Rachel labia, Jane took a piece of tissue paper and tenderly touched at the full lips until it was spotless.

As was generally the situation, Rachel stroked the young lady's head in her arms while directing her mouth straightforwardly to her protruding twat!

"OK, child, be a decent secretary and draw Jane off!" "Of all the incidental advantages this occupation advertised, "Sucking Rachels pussy was number one!"

Jane would never get enough of the over created organ, and in the wake of taking in a full breath of her inebriating smell she let her tongue crawl into the vast cut and find it's direction straightforwardly to her hard engorged clitty!!!

What was far superior was the way Rachel outlined her ideal pussy!

Rather than wearing dreary old undies, she generally wore a supporter belt combined with sheer sets of silk stockings!

Maybe her pussy was in a photo placement, and despite the fact that she was on the north side of forty years old, Rachel had the sort of body that just overflowed with sexiness!

Somewhat stout with firm legs, a full ass, adjusted stomach, practically colossal bosoms, and an exceptionally beautiful face outlined by a long mane of dull earthy colored hair!

Chapter 3

On the events when she let her pussy go to seed, a fantastic backwoods of pubic hair would cover her groin from her poop hole as far as possible up to a really wide vee and afterward to a slim path of fur dependent upon her charming navel.

It was her colossal clit, notwithstanding, that made Jane totally distraught!

At the point when it was engorged as far as possible it stood glad and solid, jabbing its glans out from between the folds of Julia's pussy for all intents and purposes asking to be sucked!

Jane was exhausted on the erect little organ, and keeping in mind that folding her tongue over its head, Rachel's body worried while a long low groan got away from her lips as a dazzling series of climaxes tweaked her pussy until it was completely spent!

"For hell's sake, sometimes you will kill me when that's what you do," Rachel moaned while the shivering in her pussy gradually died down.

"Furthermore, what a great approach," Jane chuckled while inclining up to kiss her huge titted supervisor brimming with the lips. "Mmmmmm," Julia murmured while her secretary tested her mouth with her tenacious tongue.

"I have and thought," Jane murmured, subsequent to pulling their lips apart!"

"W-what, what thought?" Rachel asked roughly. "Pick up the pace and tell me!" "It's simply this," Jane answered enthusiastically while unfastening her supervisor's white silk pullover.

"I figure it would be superb to rub our areolas together, don't you?" "Goodness yessssss," Rachel murmured unwillingly, "we should make it happen!" Each time Jane saw Rachels gigantic bosoms encased in her sheer bras was similarly essentially as energizing as the initial time, and subsequently she sucked a swallow of air and groaned delicately while stroking the huge mammaries through the lovely texture!

"L-let me see yours," Rachel heaved, "pick up the pace and take your top off!!!"

However much she cherished Rachel's chest, Jane was certain that Julia adored hers considerably more!

It was a game they never burnt out on playing, that being Jane prodding her manager with a sluggish strip bother that in a real sense stirred her into a furor!

First came the coat, then, at that point, the pullover, and afterward very leisurely the dark bra that contained her ideal 36c's!

"Jesus I love your boobs," Rachel said while touching the pink nippled ponders. "I'm certain that you do,"

Jane expressed gently while supporting up barely out of her manager's reach, "however you need to guarantee me a certain something!"

"W-what, simply let me know what you need," Rachel stammered, "anything, if it's not too much trouble, let me contact them!"

"Welllllll," Jane answered pleasantly, "it's a tiny bit of a thing." "Great fucking god, tell me!" Rachel asked.

", OK," Jane prodded while lifting the stitch of her own skirt, "it's simply this, I believe you should jerk off my clit with one of your large areolas!"

On seeing her bushy Jane was certain that Rachel would drop, however she quickly ripped off her bra and offered an enormous stub for her secretary's utilization!

A wild look covered Rachels face while she gasped, "it is right here, come and get it from mother!"

Rachel regularly pink areolas had taken on a practically purple tint as they stood apart hard as little cocks, as though asking for consideration!

Jane pussy staggered at their simple sight, and however much she needed to continue to prod her chief, she realized that opposing any more was miserable!

She moaned profoundly, and subsequent to giving Rachel a sweet young lady's grin, ventured forward with her legs spread wide apart permitting the large titted bitch to run her immense uncover and down her bushy break!

The sensation was staggering! Rachel hard nip snapped this way and that over erect clit, making an electric shock whip through her with each stroke!

Presently the situation was reversed, in a manner of speaking, and it was Julia's chance to have her direction with the cheeky twat!

While the rage in her pussy irritated her, Rachel took as much time as was needed and deliberately tried not to interface her hard areola with Jane's hard clit!

Frantically Jane attempted to move her pussy around to get positive contact, yet the wily more established lady figured out how to keep her areola barely too far!

At long last in urgency Jane snatched the fat tit from her chief and directed the energized areola where it would do the most great, straightforwardly on her destitute clit!

At the point when it happened it washed over her like a cascade as her pussy shook wild leaving her crashing on the rocks of climax city!

With her legs unbalanced and her knees powerless Jane let the enormous boob slip from her hands as she inclined vigorously against the wall for much required help!

The two ladies had the bewildered look of a deer trapped in the headlights of a semi, yet Rachel figured out how to gasp, "And that is what's truly going on with it!"

Jane dropped her skirt and started assisting Rachel with assembling herself back while murmuring, ``I surmise that will cause you to disregard Eric, huh!" "Eric who?!?" Rachel answered with a laugh.

www.ingramcontent.com/pod-product-compliance
Lightning Source LLC
Chambersburg PA
CBHW060932130726
48001CB00006B/2531